LeOn aND SAm

THE COUNTRY of RiGGleDeejurst

4   5   6½

For my mother, **Lottie Freeman**,
a woman with a sweet soul and a hero's heart.

And for **Howard**, **Jane**, and **Andrew**,
with my love.

And for **Ali Hoffman**,
who started it all.

Just As

The Story of

*For Jake.
With love,
Nancy Mark*

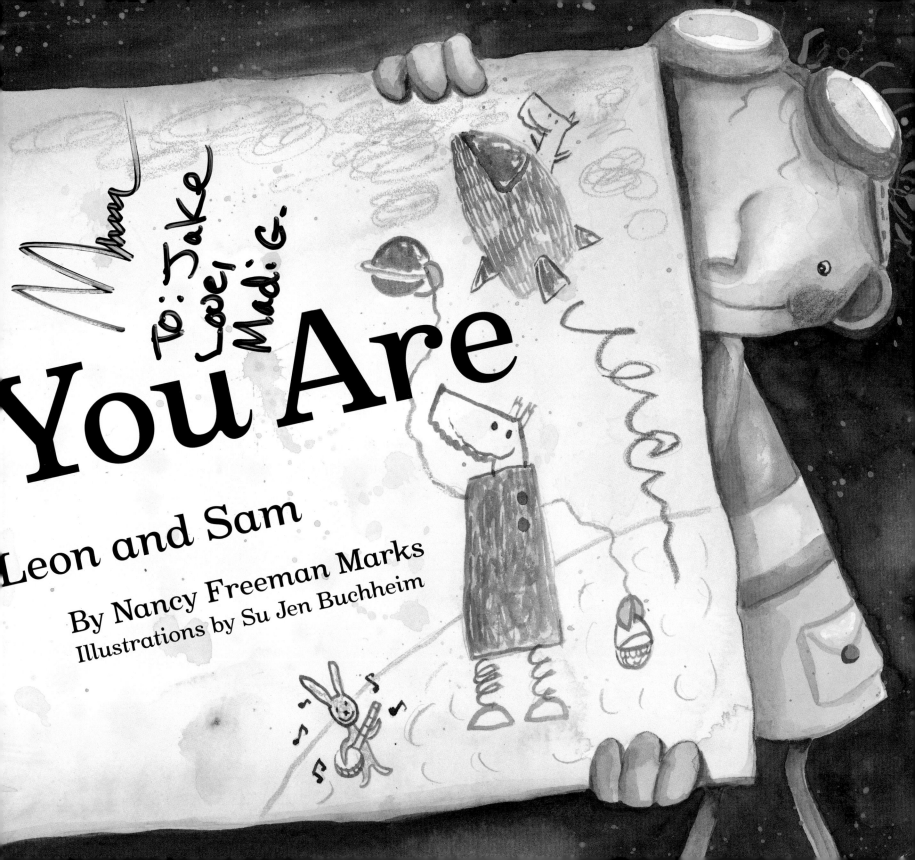

You Are

Leon and Sam

By Nancy Freeman Marks

Illustrations by Su Jen Buchheim

To: Jake
Love,
Madi. G.

Sam

Two peas-in-a-pod were the

and **Leon,** Leon and Sam,

Each loved to explore, paint bright pictures and run,
And eat pickles and popcorn all day.

This story I tell you, the interesting thing,
Is that neither knew either at **first.**
They lived near the ocean on opposite shores,

In the country of **Riggledeejurst.**

Beginning with Sam now
— first thing every day

He put

boots on right there in his bed.

He knew, when exploring, he'd need them, of course,

And they matched his pj's, which were **red.**

Well, first stop, Sam thought, as he sprang to his feet,

Was to check on the toys in his box.

Then off to the kitchen, where he docked **his boat,**

To set sail wearing waterproof socks.

His mission today – to deliver the mail
To the creatures who lived in the deep.
Sam found them in waves, under rocks and in caves –
Then he'd sing songs to help them to sleep.

For Sam was a thinker, a kind boy, a prince.
He was gentle and smart and quite **funny**.

He cared about others, small bugs
and the earth,
He was like a bright day —
clear and **sunny**.

And here's where
the story brings
Leon on in,

He's **a dog,** not a boy like our Sam.
Though his heart was the same
— that is, kind and humane —
He was cuddly and soft like a lamb.

The thing about Leon is, once long ago
He got lost from his mom and his dad.
Little Lee (that's his nickname) had nowhere to live.

He felt scared and alone and was sad.

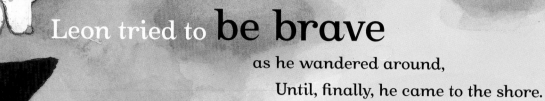

Leon tried to **be brave**

as he wandered around,

Until, finally, he came to the shore.

And guess what he saw through the fog and the mist?

It was Sam's boat

- The Wallawhatfor.

Leon barked really loud from his toes to his snout,
Thinking pirates just might be on board.

But then Sam walked the plank,
with a smile on his face,
And he tied up the boat with a cord.

So, Leon met Sam,
and Sam, Leon, of course.

Right away, **they just knew** they would be
The kind of good friends who liked play dates and snacks,

And had sleep-overs under a tree.

Next, Sam said to Leon, **"Come with me to eat,"**
Cause he saw Leon's tummy was flat.
They sat in a tepee while munching on food,
And they comfortably started **to chat.**

Their feast yummy tasted

big cheese balls and rice,

Served **with ice cream and cookies and jam.**
Leon felt really blessed in the warm, cozy tent,
With a friend as delicious as **Sam.**

"I hope Sam will like me for just who I am,
A good puppy who's funny and real.
If he does he might keep me right here in his home."
Leon thought, "That would be a great deal!"

But then, once again, Leon's sadness returned,
And he worried, "What if things I do,
Like sleep in a scarf with my feet in the air,
Make Sam say, 'I don't really like you!'"

As Sam washed the dishes, his striped bathrobe on,
Sipping apple juice mixed with V-8,

He thought, "Gee, **I like Leon.** He's really a kick.

Wonder if he can play fetch, or skate?"

"Wouldn't having a dog as a pal be such fun?

We could play tag and throw balls and yet—

What if he leaves me

or wants to go home

If I don't share my coloring set?"

The sun got to sinking,
which meant 'time for bed,'
So—Sam put his boots on the floor,
And with Leon along,
quickly jumped in their nest,

Then they both
gently started
to snore.

In their warm snuggled sleep,
each in his special way,

Began dreaming of fun things to do.
Sam pictured Leon out riding a bike.

Leon dreamed of a **clubhouse for two.**

And just as the **morning was peeking awake,**
As the moon gently slipped into bed,
The guys faced each other with smiles in **their hearts,**
And here is what each of them said:

"I love you,"
said Leon, and Sam said it back,
"Just as silly and fun as you are.
I don't care if you wear a moustache for a hat
Or save lightning bugs stuffed in a jar."

"The important thing, really,
is that you're my friend,

That I like you and that you like me.
We can twinkle the stars, fly a rocket to Mars,
What a great team we'll make, Sam and Lee!

So that's how the friendship of Leon and Sam
Started out and went on evermore.
They made mud pies, built castles, and grew straight and tall,
And were much **better friends than before.**

Both learned that each day comes with fun things to try,
And that kind words and hugs both go far.

But the best thing is having
good pals in your life,

Who will play with you **just as you are.**

For information regarding permission, please write to:
Wave Publishing, 4 Yawl Street, Venice, California 90292, 310 306-0699

Book and Jacket Design by AdamsMorioka
Master Printer, David Gardner

Library of Congress Cataloging-in-Publication Data
Marks, Nancy Freeman, 1949-
Just as you are: the story of Leon and Sam / by Nancy Freeman Marks;
illustrated by Su Jen Buchheim.
      p. cm.
Summary: Even though they come from different backgrounds, a boy named
Sam and a dog named Leon become good friends in the land of Riggledeejurst.
ISBN 0-9722430-1-1
      [1. Friendship--Fiction. 2. Dogs--Fiction. 3. Stories in rhyme.]
      I. Buchheim, Su Jen, ill. II. Title.
      PZ8.3M39175Ju 2003
      [E]--dc22
                                                          2003016874

Printed in the U.S.A.

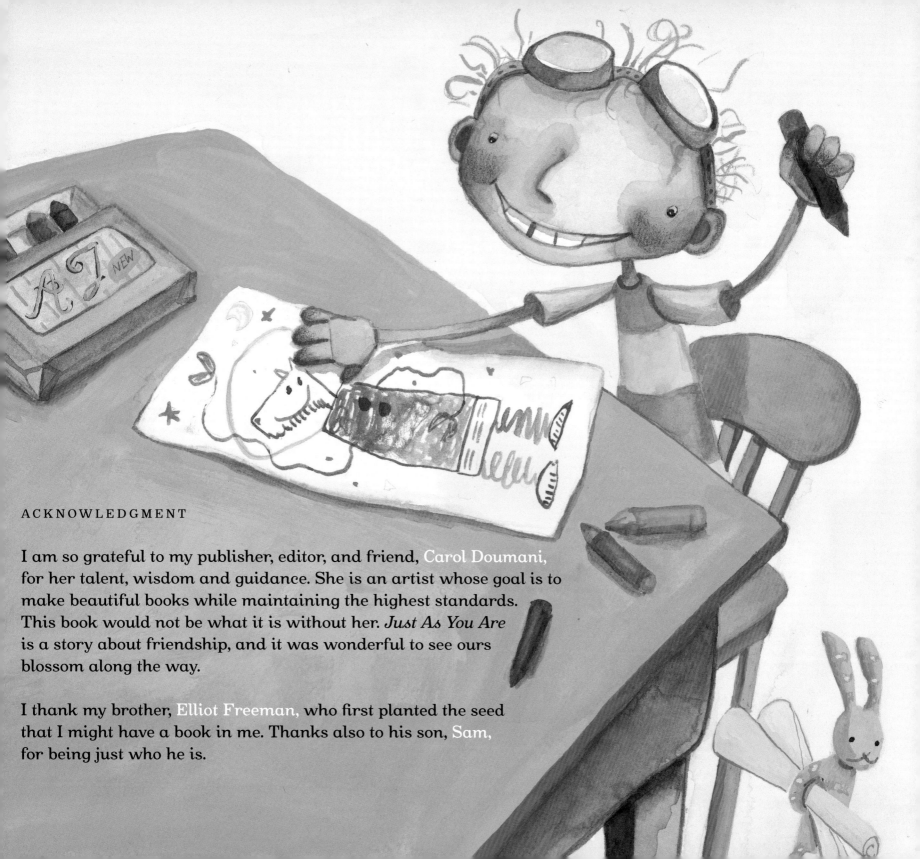

ACKNOWLEDGMENT

I am so grateful to my publisher, editor, and friend, Carol Doumani, for her talent, wisdom and guidance. She is an artist whose goal is to make beautiful books while maintaining the highest standards. This book would not be what it is without her. *Just As You Are* is a story about friendship, and it was wonderful to see ours blossom along the way.

I thank my brother, Elliot Freeman, who first planted the seed that I might have a book in me. Thanks also to his son, Sam, for being just who he is.

the Story

the Wallawhatfor

the Shore

A B C D E F G H I J K

1 2 3